I Love Mum

Joanna Walsh & Judi Abbot

SIMON AND SCHUSTER
London New York Sydney Toronto New Delhi

Some smiles are sun smiles
run for miles smiles

but no one's smile is wider, brighter,
than my **mum's** smile.

Some games are fun games but not like **Mum's** games.

She can make a paper plate
into a plane,

a couple of cups into a telephone,

a chair
into a throne,

a brolly
into a slide trombone!

But who'd have guessed
a mess could be
so quick to pick up,

a box so quick to pack up?

Count to ten, sit on the lid,
there, done!

What's next?

Nobody bakes so cake-y,

no sticky mix so yummy
(crumbs!) as much as mummy's.

But while it's in the oven
there's a dozen other bothers.

Whether it's one
or another
or all together

nobody juggles them like **Mum** till –

ting! – the baking's done!

When we go out
she slips her hand in mine.

No other mother looks so fine.

No one strolling up the street
so neat, so pretty.

And at the park nobody
swings my swing so high.

No one brings the sky
closer to the see-saw.

No one else sees
(down on our knees)
the tiny beasts creep
'cept her and me.

But if we fight

nobody else can take a wrong
and make a right.

No tears for a hurt knee or feelings
could be kissed better.

And when we set off back,
no long, long way home

so snail-slow,
could go so quick.

No hop
no skip
so slick

over our front door step –

to get us home in time for tea.

And then . . .

. . . no bath splash could be wetter.
No water jet, set to get her back,

is such a laugh.

No rub's more cuddly than **Mum's** towel hug.

No 'jamas are so warm, no bug so snuggly.

No tucking-in so dozy
no toes so cosy,
no goodnight kiss so right –

good night, **Mum**.
Good night.